Magic
Animal Friends

To Gwendolyn

Special thanks to Valerie Wilding

ISBN 978-0-545-68644-0

12 11 10 9 8 7 6 5 4 3 2 1   15 16 17 18 19 20/0

Printed in the U.S.A.   40
First printing, June 2015

Molly Twinkletail Runs Away

Daisy Meadows

Scholastic Inc.

Shining House

Sunshine Meadow

Blossom Briar

Toadstool Café

Goldie's Grotto

Toadstool Glade

Mrs. Taptree's Library

Friendship Tree

Maze

Silver Spring

Buttercup Grove

Lighthouse

Map of Friendship Forest

Ace Air Travel

Windmill

Mr. Cleverfeather's Inventing Shed

Muddlepups' Den

Treasure Tree

Sparkly Falls

Featherbills' Barge

Waterwheel

Entrance to the Caverns

Swamp

Grizelda's Tower

Can you keep a secret? I thought you could!

Then I'll tell you about an enchanted wood.

It lies through the door in the old oak tree.

Let's go there now—just follow me!

We'll find adventure that never ends,

And meet the Magic Animal Friends!

Love,
Goldie the Cat

Contents

Contents

CHAPTER ONE

A Golden Visitor

Jess Forester and her best friend, Lily Hart, were in the kitchen of the little house where Jess lived with her dad, finishing their lunch.

"I'm so full!" said Lily, patting the front of her T-shirt. "Your dad's pizzas are amazing."

Jess grinned. "It's lucky you live just across the road so you can come over whenever he makes them."

"I'm glad you enjoyed your lunch," said Mr. Forester as he came into the kitchen. "Now, what are you up to this afternoon?"

"We're going to see the animals, of course!" said Jess.

Lily's parents ran the Helping Paw Wildlife Hospital in the converted barn behind their house. Both the girls loved to help look after the animals.

"An injured fox cub came in this

morning," added Lily. "We should check on him first."

Jess nodded, making her blond curls bounce. "Good idea," she said. "That's the best thing about summer vacation— spending lots of time with the animals!"

"Wait!" said Mr. Forester. "Where do dirty plates go?"

"In the sink," chanted Lily and Jess.

As they stacked the dishes, Jess heard a soft scratching noise. "Listen," she said.

Skkks skkks skkks . . .

"It sounds like it's coming from under your sink," said Lily.

The girls crouched down to take a look. Lily pushed her bobbed dark hair behind her ears as she eased the cupboard door open. "Oh!" she whispered.

Inside was the most adorable tiny brown mouse, with ears so pink and pale the girls could almost see through them. It blinked its bright little eyes, then scurried behind the dustpan.

"It's so cute!" whispered Lily.

Mr. Forester

4

laughed. "It certainly is," he said, "but it can't stay there. We'll need to catch it!"

He rooted around in a cupboard and produced a long plastic box with a little door at one end. "See?" he said. "Once the mouse is inside, the door will close behind it. Then we can release it somewhere safe. But first," he went on, "we need something to tempt it into the box."

"Mice like chocolate," suggested Jess.

"And peanut butter!" said Lily. "Let's try some of each."

After they'd set the trap and put it back in the cupboard, the girls said good-bye to

Mr. Forester and walked across Brightley Lane to the wildlife hospital.

They passed through Lily's yard, pausing at the rabbit run. A bunny with a bandaged foot hopped slowly to the fence and gazed at them.

"Look at that snuffly little nose," Jess cooed.

Lily smiled. "He reminds me of another rabbit—little Lucy Longwhiskers! I still can hardly believe that we had an adventure in a magical forest!"

Jess nodded. "It was amazing, wasn't it?" She sighed. "All those adorable animals talking—and their cute little houses. And Goldie, too!"

Goldie was a magical cat who had once been a patient at Helping Paw. She had taken Lily and Jess into the secret world of Friendship Forest to help defeat Grizelda, a nasty witch. Grizelda wanted to drive out all the animals so she could have the forest for herself.

The girls passed the burrow Mr. and Mrs. Hart had built for the injured badgers. Next to it was a grove of trees where two fawns lay in the shade, each with a plaster cast on one leg. They stirred, blinking up at something with their long-lashed eyes.

Jess followed their gaze. There was a
flash of gold in one of the trees.

"Look!" she cried. "It's Goldie!"

A cat with golden fur darted through
the branches. She leaped down beside the
girls and they kneeled to stroke her
silky head.

"It's lovely to see you," said Lily. She turned to Jess. "Goldie said she'd find us if Grizelda was up to no good again. Is that why you're here, Goldie?"

The cat mewed, then darted toward Brightley Stream, which flowed at the bottom of the Harts' garden. She paused and looked back at the girls.

"She wants us to follow her," cried Jess. "She must be taking us back to Friendship Forest!"

Goldie jumped across the stepping-stones that crossed the stream and the girls skipped after her. They followed

Goldie to the middle of Brightley
Meadow, where a bare oak tree stood. As
the cat reached it, leaves and blossoms
sprang from its branches, bringing the tree
to life. Bees buzzed among the flowers
and birds sang from the branches.

Goldie touched a paw to the letters
carved around the trunk.

"We both have to read it, remember?"
said Lily, excitement fluttering inside her.

Jess nodded and counted, "One, two,
three . . ."

"Friendship Forest!" the girls sang out
together.

Instantly, a small door appeared in the tree trunk, as high as the girls' shoulders. Jess reached for the leaf-shaped handle and opened it. A shimmering golden light shone from inside.

With a meow, Goldie leaped through the door.

Jess grinned at Lily. "Ready?"

"You bet!" said Lily. They held hands and ducked inside, following Goldie into Friendship Forest.

CHAPTER TWO

Friendship Forest

Dazzling golden light surrounded the
girls, and their skin tingled all over. "We're
getting smaller!" said Jess.

When the light faded, the girls were in
a sun-dappled forest clearing, surrounded
by tall trees. Bright flowers nodded in the
breeze, their scents filling the air. They

gasped with delight as they saw, once
more, the little cottages that edged
Toadstool Glade.

"Welcome back," said a soft voice. Lily
and Jess turned to see Goldie smiling
at them. She was standing upright now,
and a glittery scarf was looped around
her neck. Because the girls had shrunk
slightly, their friend was almost as tall as
their shoulders.

"Goldie!" cried Lily, hugging her.

"It's even more magical than I remember," said Jess. "Look, Lily! There's the Toadstool Café!" She pointed to a little red-painted wooden building with white spots on its roof. It belonged to the Longwhiskers—a family of rabbits the girls had met when they first came to the forest.

The café door opened and a tiny rabbit came running out, her white tail bobbing behind her. "Hello, Lily, hello, Jess!" Lucy Longwhiskers hugged their ankles. "It's so nice to see you again."

"Hello, Lucy," Lily said, kneeling to stroke the little bunny. "You've got flour on your ears!"

Lucy giggled and shook her ears so the flour came off in a cloud. "I'm helping my mom and dad make seed cakes," she explained. "We've got lots more baking to do. See you soon!" With an excited squeak, she hurried back indoors.

All sorts of animals were scurrying
through Toadstool Glade, calling hello
to the girls as they passed by. A mole
waddled along with a basket of berries
over one paw, and a young hedgehog
was pushing a little wheelbarrow filled
with pine nuts, walnuts,
and sweet chestnuts.

"It's Harry
Prickleback," Jess
remembered.
"Hi, Harry!"
He waved a
paw at them.

"Goldie," Lily asked, "why did you bring us here? Is Grizelda back?"

The cat shook her golden head. "Not yet, I'm happy to say!" She smiled. "I've brought you here because there's a fair in Sunshine Meadow today. I thought you might like to come."

The girls looked at each other excitedly. "We'd love to!" Lily said.

"So that's why everyone looks so busy," exclaimed Jess. "They're getting ready for the fair!"

Harry was pushing his wheelbarrow back across the clearing. It was now filled

 18

with so many nuts that he couldn't see over the top, and his steering was off. As the girls and Goldie dodged out of Harry's way, Jess's little sketchbook fell from the pocket of her shorts.

She bent to pick it up, but a tiny golden-brown mouse got there first.

"I'll get it!" the mouse squeaked.

Lily held her breath as the mouse struggled to lift the sketchbook. *She's so small, I could hold her with just one hand*, she thought to herself.

"I'm doing it! I'm doing it!" panted the mouse. She managed to lift the book by one corner, and Jess reached down to take it. The girls kneeled beside her.

"Thank you," Jess said. "What's your name?"

"Molly," said the mouse, sitting on a tuft of moss to get her breath back. "Molly Twinkletail."

"That's a pretty name," said Lily. "You're very kind."

"I love helping people," Molly said.

"I've got a mommy and daddy and nine big brothers and sisters, and I help them all!" She twitched her whiskers. "I'm too little to help at our stall at the fair, though, so I'm helping anyone else I can. Are you hungry?" She opened her little bag and showed them what was inside. "Hazelnut chips," she said. "Try some."

Molly tipped the chips into Lily and Jess's outstretched hands. They were each the size of a grain of rice.

"Yum!" the girls said together, nibbling the chips.

"Have some more," offered Molly.

"But you won't have enough left for yourself," said Goldie.

"Don't worry," said Molly. "I'll go home and fill my bag again. All this helping is making me hungry!"

She ran to a nearby tree, scampering up the stairs carved into the trunk and onto a branch where a pretty little cottage stood. A delicious aroma wafted from its open windows.

"Will you wait and take me to Sunshine Meadow with you?" Molly called down.

"Of course," said Goldie. "Just ask your mom and dad if it's okay first."

Molly scurried indoors. A moment later,
Jess and Lily saw nine little mouse faces at
the windows. Molly's brothers and sisters!

They waved, then Molly herself ran out,
followed by a smiling mouse wearing an

apron who introduced herself to the girls as Molly's mother.

"What's that delicious smell?" asked Lily.

"We're dipping blueberries in toffee," explained Mrs. Twinkletail. "Look for us at the fair, won't you? Don't get into any trouble, Molly. Good-bye, everyone!"

Holding her bag of hazelnut chips, Molly settled happily in Lily's hands. The four friends set off for Sunshine Meadow and the fair.

CHAPTER THREE

Grizelda!

Goldie led the girls through the trees.
A bush of pale pink roses grew beside
the path and Lily stopped to admire the
delicate flowers. Molly leaned out of her
pocket and wriggled her nose.

"They smell just like my mom's
strawberry pancakes!" she squeaked.

"All the flowers look beautiful, Goldie," said Lily, looking around them. "Does that mean the Blossom Briar is better now?"

The Blossom Briar grew beside the cave where Goldie lived. As long as it was covered in blooms, all the flowers in Friendship Forest would thrive. Grizelda had tried to destroy it, but luckily the girls and Goldie had stopped her.

The cat nodded happily. "It's covered in new buds!" She led them out of the trees. "Now, here's Sunshine Meadow!"

The girls gasped as they stepped into a field of lush green grass. It was dotted with blooms of orange, yellow, and deep red.

"It's beautiful," Jess cried.

"The flowers are all the colors of sunshine," said Lily. She set Molly Twinkletail on the ground and handed her the bag of hazelnut chips.

"Thanks for the ride," said Molly. "I'm off to do some more helping. See you later!"

They waved good-bye to the tiny
mouse, and watched as the meadow
began to fill with animals preparing their
stalls and games.

Goldie pointed to where a squirrel was
setting up an apple-bobbing game—but
his apples had fallen onto the ground.
"I think Woody Flufftail needs a hand,"
she said.

They went over to Woody's stall and
helped him gather up the runaway fruit.

"These look delicious," Lily told him
as she picked up a rosy apple from under
the table.

"Here, try one!" Woody said. He held

out an apple in each paw to Lily and Jess.

"Mmm," said Jess, biting into the

crunchy fruit. "It's the best apple I've

ever tasted!"

"They're from the Treasure Tree," Woody explained. "That's where we get all our food from."

Before the girls could ask Woody more about the Treasure Tree, Lily spotted Molly scurrying toward them.

"I helped Agatha Glitterwing the magpie set out all the shiny prizes for her raffle," she said breathlessly. "And I helped Lucy Longwhiskers arrange her seed cakes."

"Goodness—" Lily began, but Molly Twinkletail took a breath and carried on.

"And I helped Mr. Cleverfeather set up his Bubble-Blower machine," she said. "He's an owl and a brilliant inventor."

The girls grinned at each other. "We met Mr. Cleverfeather last time we were here—in his inventing hut," said Jess.

"Bother!" Woody exclaimed suddenly.

"What's the matter?" asked Lily.

"I've only got big apples for my game," he said. "I completely forgot to pick small ones for the little animals!"

Molly clapped her front paws together. With an excited squeak, she scurried away again.

"Molly, where are you going?" Jess called, but the little mouse had already disappeared.

Just then, a glint of light above the forest caught Lily's eye. A glowing yellow-green orb was floating toward the meadow. The girls had seen it before, when they first came to the forest . . .

Lily felt her tummy flip over. She nudged Jess. "It looks like Grizelda has decided to join the fair, too," she said nervously.

Jess gasped. "Oh, no!"

As the orb got closer, all the animals
stopped what they were doing to
watch. When it had reached the center
of the meadow, there was a *cra-ack*
and a shower of green sparks. When
the sparks cleared, the girls saw a tall
woman in a shiny purple tunic and
tight black pants. She had cold, dark
eyes and a thin, bony nose.

"Stay back!" Goldie warned everyone.
"Grizelda the witch is here!" All the
animals squeaked in fear.

Grizelda squashed some yellow flowers

with the pointy toe of her high-heeled boot. "Well, well." She sneered. "It's the cat and her interfering humans."

"Go away, Grizelda!" Jess shouted. "Go back to your tower and leave Friendship Forest alone!"

Grizelda pointed a finger at Woody's pile of apples, and they disappeared in a puff of purple smoke. With gasps and shouts, the forest animals shrank away from her. Some of them huddled together in groups, with big ones shielding the little ones. Some were crying, and others ran to hide behind the stalls.

"The poor animals," whispered Lily. "It's the first time they've seen Grizelda. They're so frightened!"

Grizelda's eyes glittered. "Having a nice time at your little fair, are you?" she screeched. "You should be more careful. I've seen your Treasure Tree, with its silly fruit and nuts. While you're

here enjoying yourselves, my Boggits
are destroying it. Soon you won't have
anything to eat!"

The animals gasped with horror. Lily,
Jess, and Goldie looked at one another
in dismay. They'd met the Boggits—
Grizelda's filthy, horrible helpers—once
before.

"Ha-ha!" shrieked Grizelda. "You'll all
have to leave Friendship Forest and I'll
make it lovely and gloomy and move
here instead!"

The animals whimpered with fright.
Jess stepped forward. "Grizelda," she

Grizelda!

said bravely, "we stopped you before and
we'll stop you again!"

The witch glared down her pointed nose. "Think again, humans. This time there's nothing you can do to stop me!"

She snapped her fingers. With a flash and a shower of sparks, Grizelda disappeared.

CHAPTER FOUR

Ace Air Travel

Jess turned to Lily. "We need to get to
the Treasure Tree and stop those Boggits!"
she cried.

Just then, the girls heard a voice say,
"Excuse me!"

They looked around. The whole

Twinkletail family
was clustered around
their ankles!

Goldie frowned.
"Where's Molly?"
she asked the
mice.

"That's what we
came to tell you all!
We don't know!" cried Mrs. Twinkletail,
wringing her tiny paws. "We haven't
seen her all afternoon. I'm so worried
about her. It's not safe with Grizelda and
the Boggits around."

Lily thought hard. What was happening when she saw Molly scurry off? Woody had been saying that he didn't have any small apples . . .

"Oh, no!" she cried. "I think Molly's gone to the Treasure Tree to collect apples for Woody."

Jess groaned. "But that's where the Boggits are!"

The Twinkletail family squeaked with panic.

"What if the Boggits snatch her?" said Mrs. Twinkletail, her whiskers quivering. "Oh, dear, oh, dear! My poor little Molly!"

Jess and Lily looked anxiously at Goldie. She nodded as if she could tell what they were thinking.

"We'll find Molly, Mrs. Twinkletail," Goldie said. "We'll bring her home safely, I promise!"

Goldie took hold of the girls' hands and led them across Sunshine Meadow.

"I know a way to get to the Treasure Tree in no time," she said. "Come with me!"

On the other side of the meadow, they found a tall stork wearing a flying helmet with a badge that read ACE AIR TRAVEL.

"It's Captain Ace!" said Lily. "We met him the last time we came to Friendship Forest."

Goldie quickly explained the situation to Ace. "Will you give us a ride to the Treasure Tree, Captain?"

"Ace Air Travel at your service," said the stork, saluting. "Follow me!"

They hurried to a small grassy clearing. In the middle were two wooden benches.

Lily grinned. "This must be Ace Air Travel's departure lounge," she said.

The stork gave a small cough. "Ahem. Look up, please, young misses . . ."

Floating above the trees was a brightly

colored patchwork hot-air balloon.

"Wow!" said Jess. "Are we flying

in that?"

Goldie grinned. "We are."

Ace untied a rope from a peg in
the ground and pulled. Down came the
balloon's basket, low enough for the girls
and Goldie to climb in.

Ace pulled a cord that dangled down
into the basket. *Whoosh!* A stream of
bubbles shot up into the open mouth
of the balloon.

"It runs on bubble power," Ace
explained. "Mr. Cleverfeather invented it
for me. Ready for takeoff?"

"Yes!" the girls and Goldie cried.

The stork saluted again. "Knots away!"

Molly Twinkletail

he called, untying a second rope and freeing the balloon. The basket bounced gently, then drifted upward.

Ace's great wings rose and fell lazily as he flew

alongside the balloon with the rope in his beak. Goldie and the girls looked down over the treetops. It was like a sea of green, yellow, and gold.

"Look, we're just passing Sparkly Falls," said Goldie, pointing to a beautiful waterfall.

Jess looked down at the flash of sparkling blue amid the greenery. "I wish I had time to sketch it! Oh, isn't Friendship Forest beautiful?"

With a tilt of his wings, Ace changed
the balloon's direction. Ahead was an
enormous tree that towered above the rest
of the forest.

"And there's the Treasure Tree!" said
Goldie. "I wonder if Molly's gotten
there yet?"

Lily's eye was caught by a glimpse of
sickly yellow among the Treasure Tree's
branches. It looked like dirty, mud-stained
fur, and she'd seen it before . . . "Boggits!"
she cried.

CHAPTER FIVE

Trouble at the Treasure Tree

"Poor Molly might already be down
there," said Lily. "If she's run into the
Boggits, she'll be so scared."

As they got closer to the Treasure Tree,
the girls saw that it was much taller
than all the other trees, and its leaves

shimmered in the sunshine. Different kinds of fruit and nuts covered its branches. There were apples and oranges, raspberries and strawberries, spiky pineapples and plump peaches. Nuts hung among the fruit in shiny clusters.

"Wow," said Jess with a gasp. "It's amazing!"

"And the Boggits are ruining it," Goldie said grimly. "Look!" She pointed to where two of the Boggits had climbed onto one of the lower branches. One of them was ripping off fruit and throwing it onto the ground while another Boggit was yanking on a higher branch. It snapped off with a crack. The Boggit used the broken branch to whack more fruit from the tree.

"Oh, no," said Lily in dismay. "The more damage they do, the less food there will be for all the animals. We've got to stop those Boggits!"

Goldie called to Captain Ace. "Can you set us down somewhere the Boggits won't see us?"

Ace steered the balloon behind a small hill that was covered in flowering bushes. He lowered the basket and flipped a rope ladder over the side.

The passengers climbed down to the forest floor. "Thanks for the ride!" they said, keeping their voices low so the Boggits wouldn't hear.

"You're welcome," whispered Captain Ace with another salute. "Good luck, Goldie. Good luck, young misses!" He took the rope in his beak and flew silently away.

Goldie led the girls around the hill, creeping from tree to tree. As they got closer to the Treasure Tree, Jess noticed some crumbs on the ground. She looked down.

"Hazelnut chips!" she said softly. "Molly's definitely here somewhere. I hope the Boggits haven't noticed her!"

"We'd better make sure we find her first," whispered Lily.

They peeked out from behind a tree trunk. The Treasure Tree was shaking as the Boggits clambered up its branches. They were as tall as the girls, and wore ragged, filthy clothes. Their rough fur was colored in patches of dingy green, washed-out blue, and sickly yellow, and it was matted

with dried mud. They stank of rotting
cauliflowers.

The Boggits were so busy ruining
the tree they didn't realize they were
being watched.

"Haargh haargh!" Sniff laughed from
up where she squatted on a branch, her
mouth open so wide the girls could see all
her dirty teeth. "If Boggits chuck down
silly fruit they go smashed and muddy
and covered in ants!"

"Hegga hegga!" Reek chuckled.
"Grizelda will be pleased with Boggits
for ruining animals' food."

Whiffy spun around, flinging peaches in all directions. "Grizelda will laugh when Boggits tell her about silly little mouse who wanted to help Boggits, too!"

Jess and Lily both drew a sharp breath. They must be talking about Molly!

Pongo thumped his chest. "Pongo was clever, telling her to fetch drinks from Sparkly Falls for Boggits."

Sniff laughed so much she nearly fell out of the tree. "Off mouse run to help. But mouse will never be able to do it. Haargh haargh!"

The Boggits whooped and jumped onto the ground. They ran around the Treasure Tree trunk, kicking squashed fruit at each other.

Jess, Lily, and Goldie stared at one another in alarm.

"Poor Molly," said Lily. "She just wants to help people—even the horrible Boggits. Now she's even farther from home. And all alone!"

"At least we know where to find her," said Jess. "Goldie, how do we get to Sparkly Falls?"

Goldie was already heading back around the flowering bushes. "It's this way, girls! I know a shortcut."

The two friends set off after the cat. "Once we've rescued Molly," Jess said, "we'll work out a way to stop the Boggits from ruining the Treasure Tree."

"But we've got to hurry," said Lily. "Soon the poor animals won't have any food left!"

CHAPTER SIX

The Paddlefoots

Goldie led the way through the forest, turning onto a sloping stony path.

Suppose Molly falls into the waterfall? Lily thought. *Can she swim?*

Jess looked worried, too. They hurried along the path even more quickly, toward the roar of the waterfall.

They turned a corner and suddenly, right in front of them, there was a sparkling, rushing curtain of water. It tumbled over a steep rock face, foaming and bubbling as it crashed into the pool below.

"Sparkly Falls!" gasped Lily. "It's beautiful!"

"And dangerous," said Goldie quickly. "Watch where you step. The water makes everything slippery."

They clambered over rocks, getting as

close to the waterfall
as possible.

"The spray's soaking
us!" Jess shouted over the
water's roar. "Molly must
be so frightened." She
cupped her hands around
her mouth and called,
"Molly!"

"Molly Twinkletail!"
echoed Lily.

Goldie darted from rock to rock. "Where can she be?" she said anxiously. "Little Molly will be hard to spot."

"Look!" yelled Lily. "There's a dark patch behind the waterfall—I think it's a cave."

"It is!" cried Jess. "And there's Molly!"

Lily couldn't see her at first, but as the water swished and poured she suddenly made out the little mouse's shape. She was running from side to side in panic.

"Molly, don't be frightened," Lily called. "We'll get you out of there!"

Jess ran over to the jagged rocks at

the side of the falls and began to climb,
hoping to get behind the curtain of
water. But suddenly she slipped and
fell, sliding down toward the foaming,
swirling pool beneath!

"Jess!" yelled Lily, her dark eyes
wide with horror.

She and Goldie lunged toward Jess as
she slithered past. Goldie stretched out a
paw to grab her, and together she and
Lily pulled Jess to safety.

"Thanks." Jess gasped. Her heart was
hammering with fright.

"Let me try to reach Molly," said Lily,
but Goldie stopped her.

"It's too dangerous," Goldie said,
pointing at the churning water. "If you
fall in, you'll be swept away."

Lily felt tearful. "Then what can
we do?" She groaned. "If only we
could slow the water down, we could

get behind it and rescue Molly from
the cave."

"That's it!" Goldie cried. "And I know
who can help. Come on!"

"Don't worry, Molly. We'll be back!"
Jess yelled, then she and Lily followed the
cat upstream. Goldie stopped beside a
little yellow cottage with a waterwheel
outside.

"Who lives here?" asked Lily.

"The Paddlefoots," said Goldie,
knocking on the door.

A moment later the door opened and a
family of beavers rushed out. They were

wearing boots, and between them they
carried rugs and several picnic baskets.

"Goldie!" the beavers cried. "What a
lovely surprise!"

"This is Mr. and Mrs. Paddlefoot,"
Goldie said, "their children Bobby
and Betsy, and Grandpa and
Grandma Paddlefoot."

"And you must be Jess and Lily!" said Mrs. Paddlefoot. "We've heard all about you, haven't we, children?"

Bobby and Betsy bounced excitedly. "You beat Grizelda!" they chanted.

"Quiet, little ones," said Mr. Paddlefoot. "Goldie, we're off to the fair. Aren't you three going, too?"

Goldie quickly explained about Molly. "We need your help, Mr. Paddlefoot. If you could build a dam to block the waterfall, we could rescue her."

The adult beavers dropped everything. "Ready and willing we are, Goldie," said

Mr. Paddlefoot. "The Twinkletails are old friends of ours."

"Bobby and Betsy will help, too, won't you, children?" added Mrs. Paddlefoot.

"Yay!" they cried.

Mrs. Paddlefoot chose a spot a little upstream, so their cottage wouldn't be flooded when water built up behind the dam. Lily and Jess ran back downstream and shouted their plan to Molly over the thunder of the waterfall. The little mouse nodded her head to show she'd understood.

"We'll save you as soon as we can," Jess yelled. "We promise!"

The girls and Goldie helped the beaver family gather sticks, twigs, and stones, which Mr. and Mrs. Paddlefoot then put across the stream to start the dam. The two grandparents packed mud between the twigs to hold them together.

"How will the dam work, Goldie?" Jess asked, dropping another load of branches on top of the growing pile.

"Water will build up behind the dam instead of flowing down toward the waterfall," Goldie explained. "The thick branches will support it at the front."

Soon the dam had almost blocked the stream, and a pool had formed behind it.

"Go and check the waterfall, please, girls," called Mr. Paddlefoot. "It should have almost stopped."

Lily and Jess ran to the waterfall. The rush of water had slowed to just a trickle.

Jess jumped up and down in excitement. "The dam's working!" she yelled.

Lily cheered. "Now we can save Molly!"

CHAPTER SEVEN

The Sparkly Falls Plan

Lily and Jess clambered down the slope to where the curtain of water had been falling before.

"Molly!" Lily cried.

The little mouse was shivering inside the cave. The girls climbed over the rocks toward her, easily keeping their balance now that they didn't have to fight against the waterfall.

Molly gave a delighted squeak as Jess picked her up. "You s-s-s-saved me!" she said, her tiny teeth chattering with cold.

"You're safe now," murmured Lily, stroking Molly's little pink ears.

The girls climbed back to the water's edge, where Goldie and the whole Paddlefoot family gave a big cheer.

"Here," said Goldie, taking her scarf off. "Wrap Molly in this."

Lily wrapped Molly in the scarf and cuddled her against her chest. She could feel Molly stop shivering as the little mouse warmed up.

Jess spotted Molly's bag of hazelnut chips on the river bank and picked it up.

"I left them there so they wouldn't get wet," explained the little mouse. "Help yourself. It's the only way I can thank you for saving me."

Everyone was delighted that Molly

was safe. But Lily noticed that Molly's whiskers were drooping.

"What's the matter?" she asked.

The little mouse sighed. "I was trying to help those hairy creatures by fetching them a drink of water from Sparkly Falls," she said. "I saw Jenny Littlefeather the wren and she flew me here on her back. But after Jenny flew off, I got stuck behind the water. The creatures will be so thirsty."

"Molly," said Goldie, "those hairy creatures are Boggits and they were playing a cruel trick on you."

"Oh, no!" squeaked Molly, covering her eyes with her tiny paws.

"It's okay," said Lily gently. "We won't let them do it again."

"We'd better get back to the Treasure Tree," said Goldie, "before the Boggits ruin all the food."

Jess was looking thoughtfully at where the waterfall had been. "You know the Boggits love being dirty and smelly," she said slowly. "Well, maybe we can use all the water behind the dam to make them so lovely and clean that they forget about ruining the Treasure Tree."

"Good idea, Jess!" said Lily. "But how can we get the Boggits to come to Sparkly Falls?"

Everyone thought hard. Suddenly, Goldie grinned.

"I've got just the plan. We'll send them a message!"

"But how?" Lily asked.

"Easy," Goldie said. "We just need a flyer."

She made a butterfly shape with her paws, and fluttered them like wings. Instantly, a purple butterfly darted along the riverbank and came to rest on a nearby flower.

"Hello!" said the butterfly's tiny, tinkly voice.

Jess and Lily were thrilled. A talking butterfly!

"This is Hermia," said Goldie. "She and her friends deliver messages for all the animals. Hermia, are you brave enough to take a flyer to the Boggits?"

The butterfly's wings turned pale and droopy. "I'll be brave," she said, "if it helps stop them from hurting the Treasure Tree."

Jess grinned. "Thank you, Hermia. I know just the kind of message we should send . . ."

She pulled her sketchbook from her pocket, flipped it open, and began to write.

Lily peered over her shoulder. "'Dear Boggits,'" she read. "'You've done enough good work ruining the Treasure Tree. It looks truly terrible. Now go to Sparkly Falls and chuck lots of mud and garbage in the water. It's disgustingly clean. From Grizelda.'"

Everyone grinned.

"That should do the trick," said Jess. She rolled up the note and held it out so Hermia could carry it.

"Good luck, Hermia!" the girls cried as the butterfly fluttered away.

Lily turned to the Paddlefoots. "When

the Boggits get here, can you pull the
dam away?"

Mrs. Paddlefoot rubbed her paws. "It
will be our pleasure to help teach those
Boggits a lesson, won't it, everyone?" she
said to her family. "Let's get in position by
the dam and stay out of sight."

"We won't move until you give us the
signal!" Mr. Paddlefoot said to the girls.

The beavers hurried back to the dam, while Lily, Jess, and Goldie lay down on the grass at the top of Sparkly Falls. Molly sat beside them, sharing her hazelnut chips as they waited for the Boggits to arrive.

They all froze as they heard the sound of stomping, stamping feet, and the rough, gruff voices of the Boggits.

"They got Hermia's message," said Goldie.

They watched the Boggits come out of the forest, staring and scratching their grubby heads.

"Water be gone," said Pongo. "Where be the water?"

"Boggits find out," said Reek with a growl.

The four hairy creatures stepped onto the rocks.

"Now!" shouted Lily and Jess.

CHAPTER EIGHT

A Bath for the Boggits

Mr. Paddlefoot gave the girls a thumbs-up,
then the beavers rolled away the logs that
supported the dam.

Whoosh!

Jess and Lily watched in amazement
as a torrent of water gushed all over

the shrieking Boggits. Molly's whiskers
twitched with excitement.

The Boggits roared and gasped as
they tried to escape the downpour. They
stumbled and spluttered, sliding over the
slippery rocks in their panic to get to
dry land.

But when they got there, they had another shock.

They were clean! All the mud and filth had been washed away, and their multi-colored fur was gleaming.

"Boggits is wet," Sniff said with a shiver. "Lovely mud has gone. Boggits is cold."

"Urgh!" grunted Pongo. "Boggits must get muddy again."

Whiffy squeezed water from her skirt, wailing, "Whiffy's clothes is clean and nasty." She bent over and gave a horrified bellow. "Whiffy's *skirt* is clean!"

Reek charged into the trees. "Run!
Boggits must go back to Grizelda's tower
and get in mud pool!" he roared.

The others crashed after him through
the forest.

"Hooray!" shouted the girls and
their animal friends. Molly Twinkletail
squeaked and clapped her tiny paws.

Goldie grinned. "The Boggits will be so
busy getting dirty again that they'll forget
all about the Treasure Tree," she said. "And
I've got an idea for how we can fix the
mess they've made . . ."

A little while later, all the animals had helped move the fair from Sunshine Meadow to the area around the Treasure Tree. Woody Flufftail and the other animals were upset when they saw how many nuts and pieces of fruit the Boggits had pulled from the tree.

"Don't worry," Goldie said. "There's still enough left for everyone to have plenty of food. The fruit and nuts will grow back."

Then Goldie explained her plan.

"We can change all the games so that everyone helps to clean up the mess the Boggits made," she told the animals, "but has fun at the same time."

"I know!" said Jess. "We could make a bottle toss with all the nuts the Boggits chucked around."

"And have a game where whoever collects the most squashed fruit wins," Lily suggested.

Woody and all of the other animals exchanged grins. "Fantastic!" they all said.

"Give some of the foiled soot—

I mean, spoiled fruit—to me," said Mr. Cleverfeather, adjusting his monocle. "I've got an idea . . ."

Soon everyone was enjoying themselves. Jess and Lily looked after the squashed-fruit-collecting competition, where Harry Prickleback was collecting apples by curling into a ball and rolling around, spiking the fruit on his spines. Molly and her nine brothers and sisters were squeaking happily as they danced in the bubbles pouring from Mr. Cleverfeather's Bubble-Blower machine. He was tipping squashed fruit into it

to make multicolored bubbles. They smelled delicious when they popped!

"I didn't manage to get the apples Woody needed for apple-bobbing," Molly told the girls, "but this is much more fun!"

As the sun began to set, the squashed fruit and nuts had been cleared away.

"Thank you," Woody said to the girls and Goldie, his tail swishing happily. "There would be nothing growing on the tree at all if it wasn't for you."

Mr. and Mrs. Twinkletail each hugged the girls. "Thank you again for saving our Molly," Mr. Twinkletail said.

Lily and Jess said
good-bye to Molly
and all their
other friends,
then Goldie took
them back to
the magical tree
in the center of
the forest so they
could return to their
own world. She touched the trunk with
her paw and a door appeared.

"I'm so happy you were here today to
stop Grizelda!" said the golden cat.

"So are we!" agreed Lily. "Do you think she'll try to drive out all the animals again?"

"I'm sure she will," Goldie said. "And when she's back, I'll come and get you."

Jess and Lily hugged her.

"See you soon," said Jess.

"Knowing Grizelda, you won't have to wait very long!" said Goldie.

The girls stepped through the door and into the golden light that shimmered inside. A moment later, they found themselves in Brightley Meadow.

"Wow," said Lily, rubbing her eyes.

"That was an amazing adventure. I'm so glad we found Molly."

"And saved the Treasure Tree," said Jess with a smile.

They skipped back over the stepping stones. "Let's go to your house and check on the other little mouse," Lily said.

But when they asked Mr. Forester if

he'd looked at the trap yet, he looked confused. "Of course not. You've only been gone ten minutes."

Lily and Jess giggled. They'd forgotten that time stood still when they were in Friendship Forest!

"I'll check it," said Jess.

She looked in the cupboard. "Lily!" she whispered. "The trap's little door is shut."

"The mouse must be in there," Lily said.

Jess picked up the trap. She could hear something moving inside. "Let's set it free," she said.

She carefully carried the trap to the

trees at the end of the garden and set it down. Lily lifted the little door.

A moment later a tiny nose appeared, and slowly, slowly, the little brown mouse crept out. It scampered across the grass to a nearby hazel tree. There it stopped to nibble a fallen nut.

Lily and Jess smiled.

"Hazelnuts must be its favorite snack," said Jess.

Lily laughed. "Just like Molly Twinkletail!"

The End

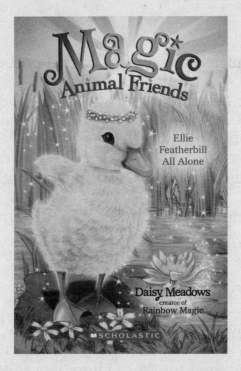

Grizelda is still causing trouble in Friendship Forest and now her Boggits are planning to poison the river! Can Lily and Jess stop them?

Find out in their next adventure,

Ellie Featherbill All Alone

Turn the page for a sneak peek ...

Lily kneeled to comfort Mrs. Featherbill. "We've come to help," she said. "We won't let the Boggits win."

"One, two, three . . ." said Mr. Featherbill, counting his ducklings. "No . . . One, two . . . Keep still, children. One, two, three, four . . ."

"Don't worry," said Lily. "I counted them as they landed. There are seven."

"Seven?" cried Mrs. Featherbill. "There should be eight! Who's missing?" She waddled around the ducklings. "There's Lulu and Dilly, Stanley and Rodney," she said. "Keep still, children. There's

Betsy, Bobo, and Sunny. Oh, no! Where's Ellie?"

Lily gasped. "She must still be on the barge—with the Boggits!"

Read

Ellie Featherbill
All Alone

to find out what happens next!

Puzzle Fun!

Can you unscramble the letters below to find
the names of five characters in this book?

ILLY RATH

BOYBB DADPLETOOF

JSSE ROFTERES

LOGIDE

MLLOY WINTLEKLAIT

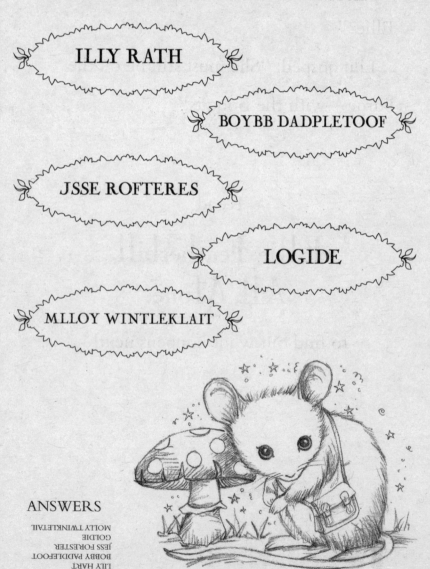

ANSWERS